6/98

To Pop, with love.

K.W.

Henry Holt and Company, Inc.

Publishers since 1866

115 West 18th Street

New York, New York 10011

Henry Holt is a registered trademark of Henry Holt and Company, Inc.

Text copyright © 1996 by Karen Wallace

Illustrations copyright © 1996 by Mike Bostock

Published by arrangement with Hodder Children's Books

The author and/or illustrator asserts the moral right

to be identified as the author and/or illustrator of this work.

First published in the United States in 1997 by

Henry Holt and Company, Inc.

Originally published in England in 1996 by Hodder Children's Books

Library of Congress Catalog Card Number: 95-81070

ISBN 0-8050-4637-2

First American Edition—1997

1 3 5 7 9 10 8 6 4 2

Printed in Singapore

Imagine You Are a
CROCODILE

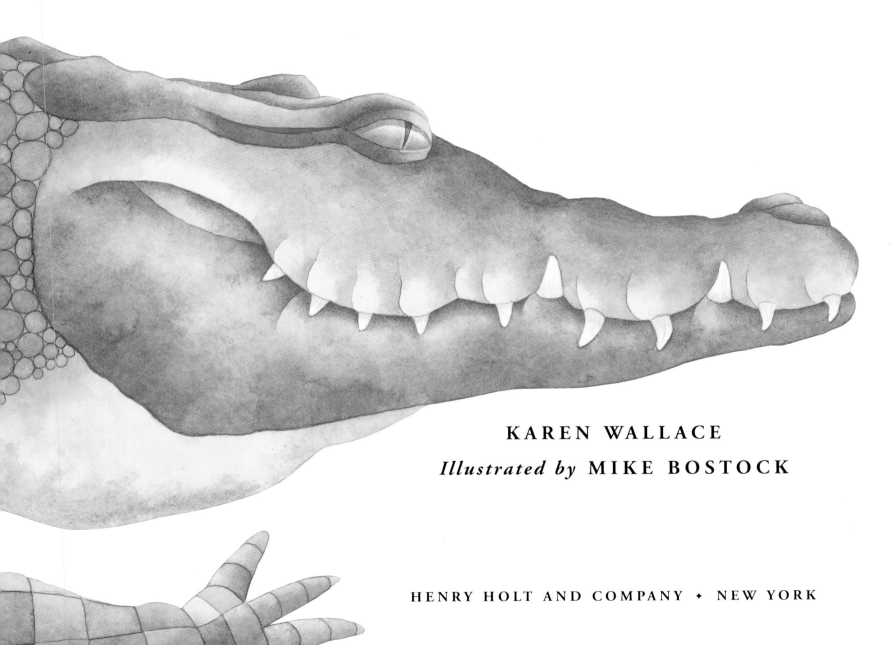

KAREN WALLACE

Illustrated by MIKE BOSTOCK

HENRY HOLT AND COMPANY ◆ NEW YORK

Imagine you are a crocodile.

A huge, hungry crocodile lies in a swamp.
The swamp is murky and green.
Flies buzz in the sunshine.

The crocodile hangs in the water
like a rotten log. Her two yellow eyes
seem to float on the scum.

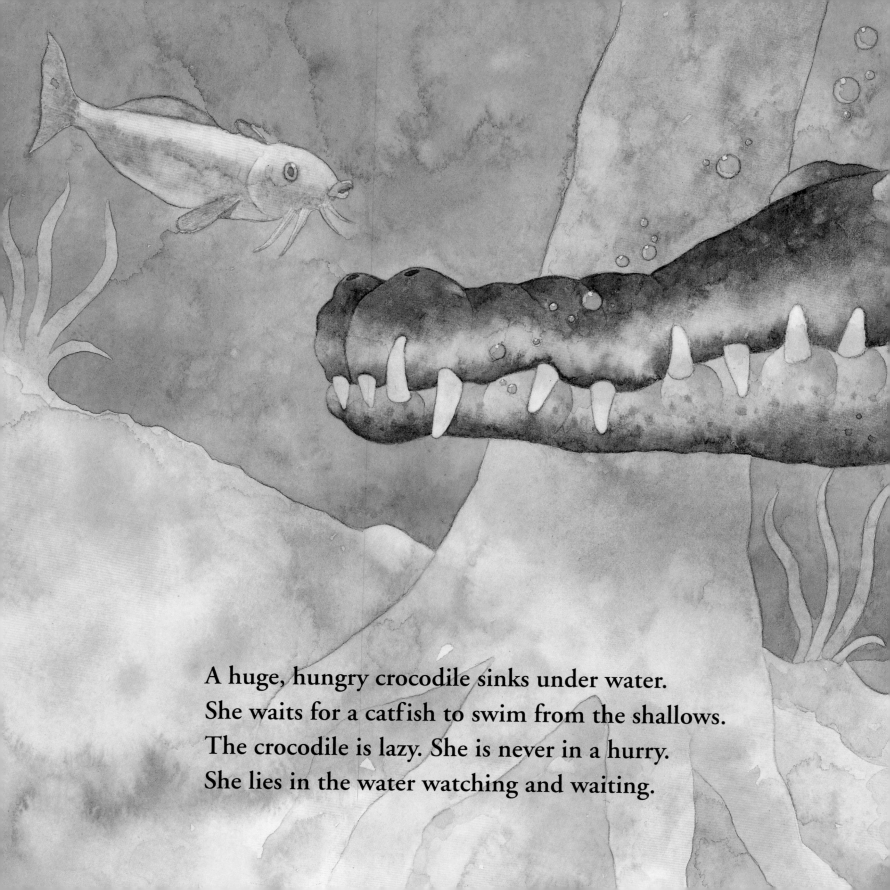

A huge, hungry crocodile sinks under water.
She waits for a catfish to swim from the shallows.
The crocodile is lazy. She is never in a hurry.
She lies in the water watching and waiting.

Imagine you are a crocodile,
a jaw-snapping crocodile.
Suddenly a heron flies over the swamp.
The crocodile jumps.
She seems to stand on the water,
and snatches the heron
as it flies past her snout.

Imagine you are a crocodile, a full-bellied crocodile.
She turns in the water and glides to the bank.
Other crocodiles are resting. She climbs in among them.

The crocodile yawns.
Her mouth is huge as a cave.
Small birds peck for food
between her sharp teeth.
She closes her eyes
and sleeps in the sun.

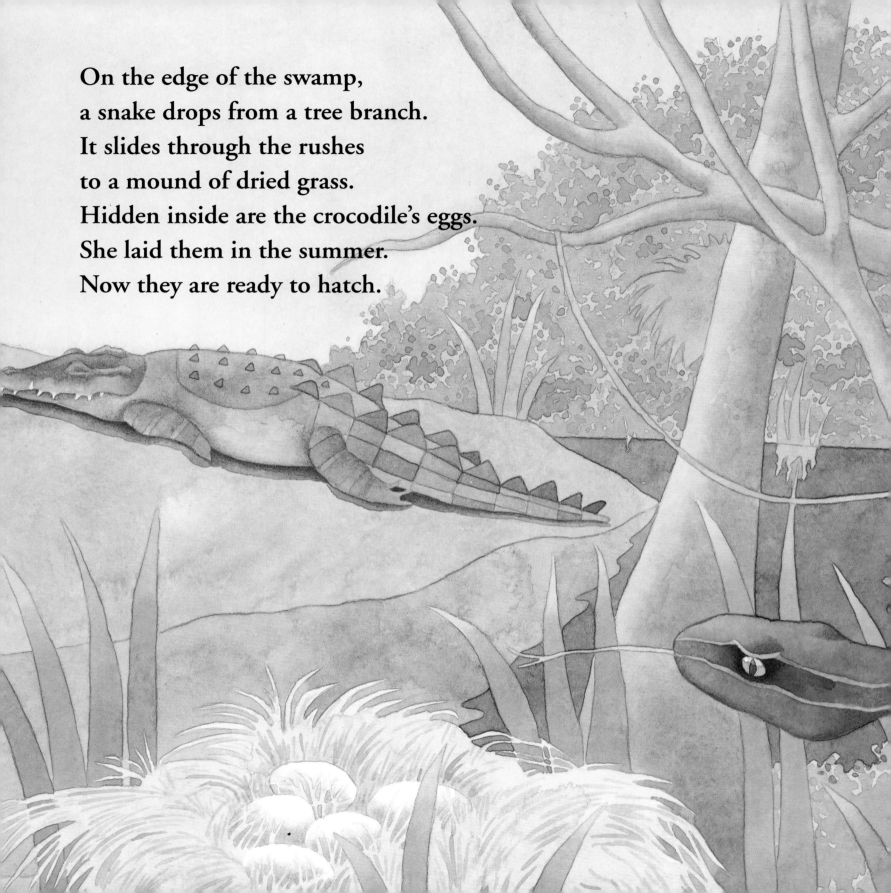

On the edge of the swamp,
a snake drops from a tree branch.
It slides through the rushes
to a mound of dried grass.
Hidden inside are the crocodile's eggs.
She laid them in the summer.
Now they are ready to hatch.

Imagine you are a crocodile asleep in the sunshine.

The sound of tiny barks floats across the rushes.

Inside their eggs, her babies are calling.

The snake slithers closer.

The crocodile wakes.

She plows through the reeds,
clambers onto her nest.
Then she digs out the eggs
with her short stubby claws.
Imagine you are a crocodile,
a fierce mother crocodile.
Her babies poke through their shells
and squeeze themselves out.

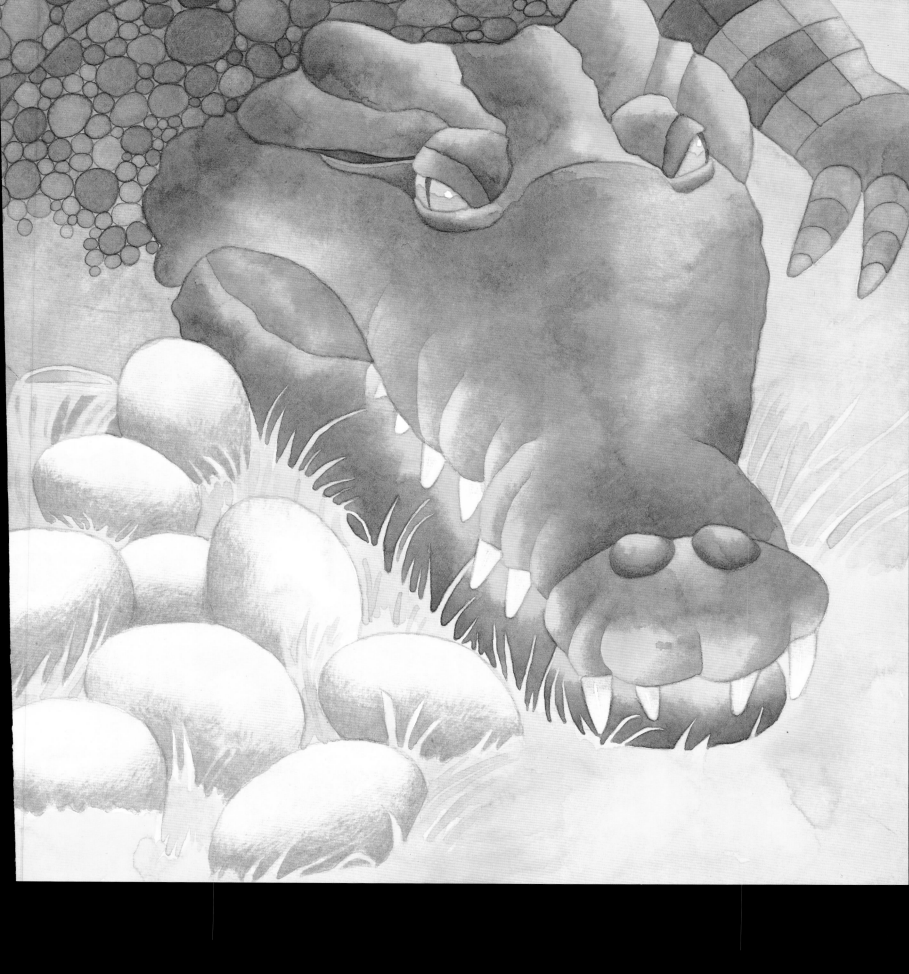

She carries them in her mouth
down to the water. Her babies are tiny
but their teeth are like needles.
They learn to catch flies
and crack open beetles.

Imagine you are a crocodile, a watchful mother crocodile.
In the night when the swamp is steamy and black,
other crocodiles hunt like wolves in the water.
In the darkness an owl hoots.
A lizard rustles in the grass.
Mother crocodile keeps her babies safely beside her.

A long, scaly crocodile lies on a mudbank.
Her skin is her armor.
Her teeth are her weapons.
She looks like a dragon asleep in the sun.

Imagine you are a crocodile.